nerod's

with love

For Susan Pearson

Copyright © 1994 by Jan Ormerod. All rights reserved. No part of this book may be reproduced or utilized in any form or by any means, electronic or mechanical, including photocopying and recording, or by any information storage and retrieval system, without permission in writing from the Publisher. Inquiries should be addressed to Lothrop, Lee & Shepard Books, a division of William Morrow & Company, Inc., 1350 Avenue of the Americas, New York, New York 10019. Printed in Singapore.

First Edition   1 2 3 4 5 6 7 8 9 10

Library of Congress Cataloging in Publication Data
Ormerod, Jan. Jan Ormerod's To baby with love/by Jan Ormerod. p. cm. Summary: An illustrated collection of traditional nursery rhymes, including "Two Little Dicky Birds," "Turtle," and "What Are We to Do?" ISBN 0-688-12558-1.—ISBN 0-688-12559-X (lib. bdg.) 1. Nursery rhymes. 2. Children's poetry. [1. Nursery rhymes.] I. Title. II. Title: To baby with love. PZ8.3.0718Jan 1994 398.8—dc20 93-8093 CIP AC

• Jan Ormerod's •

to baby with love

Lothrop, Lee & Shepard Books   New York

CONTENTS

· What Are We to Do? ·

A dog

can guard the house.

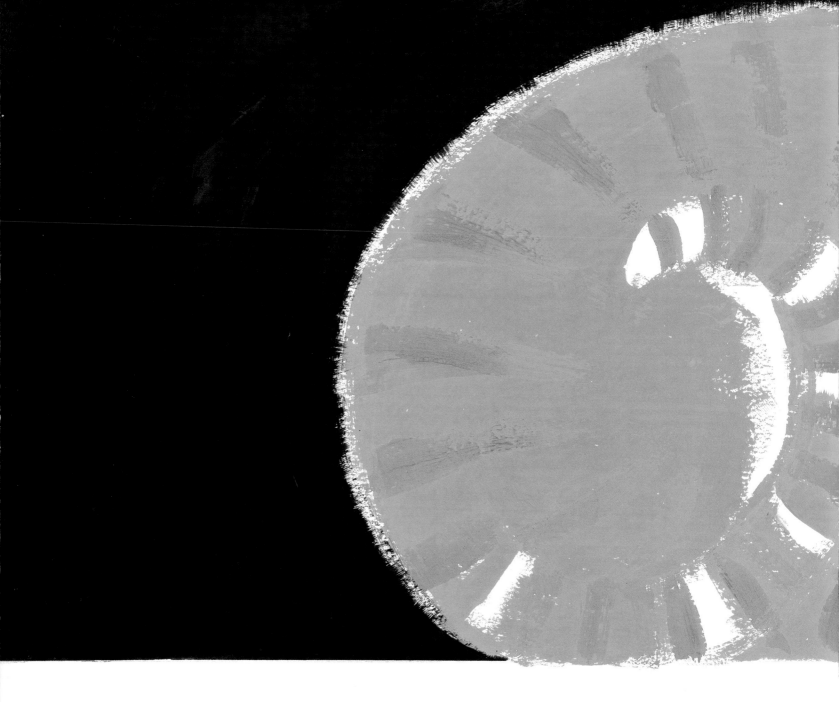

A cat

can catch a mouse.

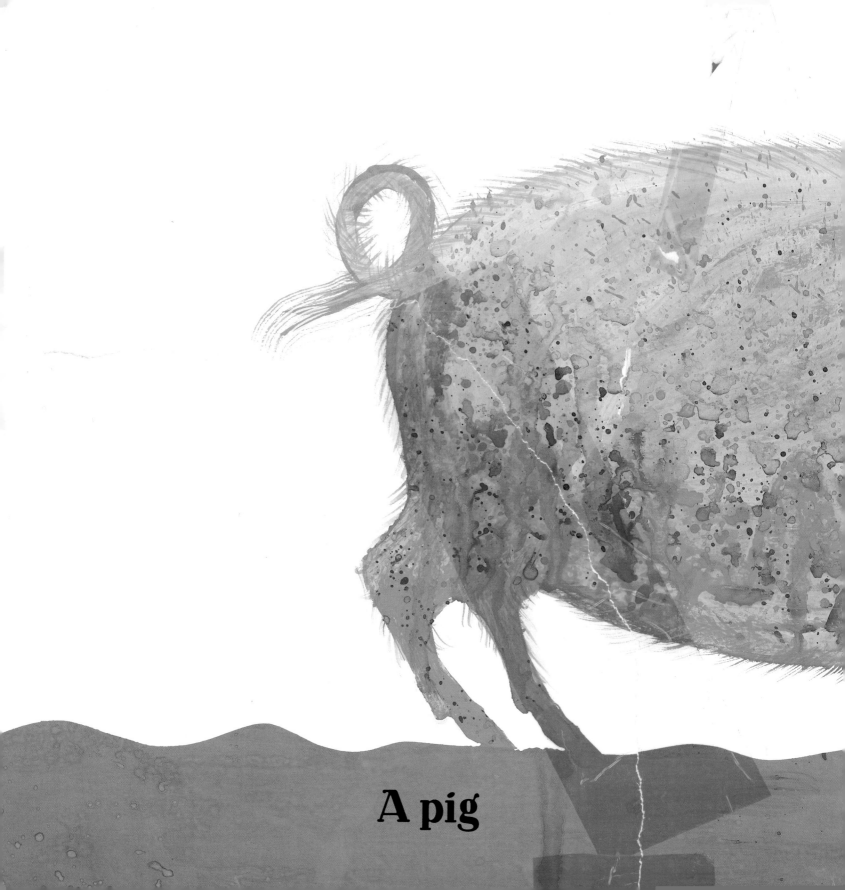

A pig

is lots of use.

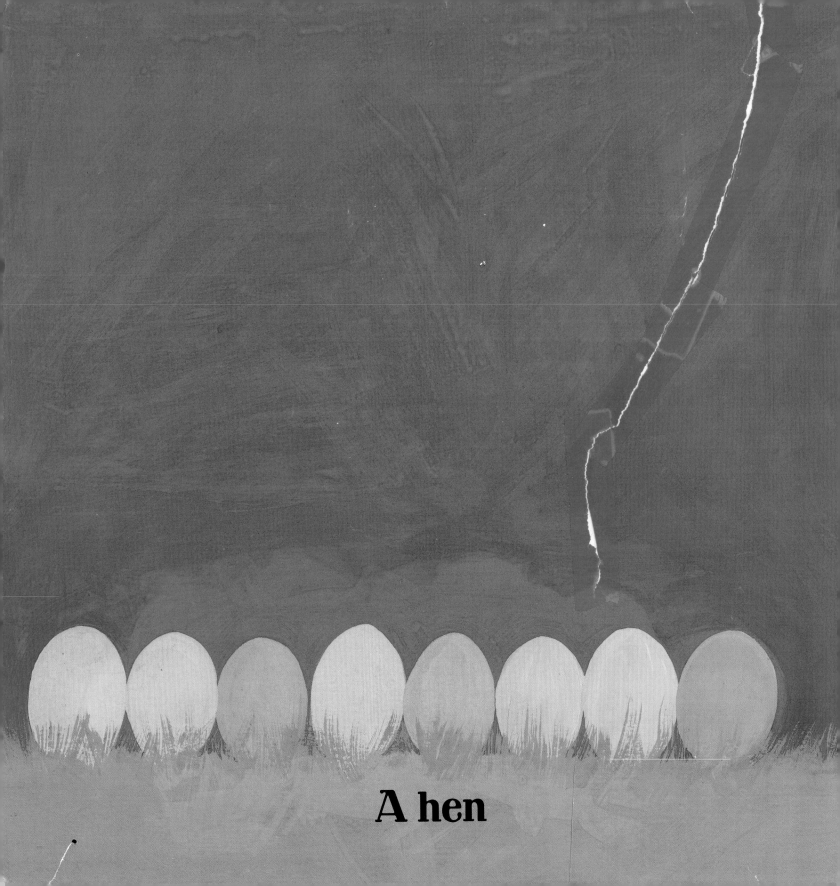

A hen

needs no excuse.

But what

are we to do...

with a little one

like you?

Two Little Dicky Birds

Two little dicky birds
sitting on a wall,

one named Peter,
the other named Paul.

Fly away, Peter.

Fly away, Paul.

Come back, Peter.

Come back, Paul.

· Chickens ·

Cluck, cluck, cluck, cluck.

**Good morning, Mrs. Hen.
How many chickens have you got?**

Madam, I have ten.

Four of them

are yellow.

And four of them

are brown.

And two of them are speckled red—

the sweetest chicks in town.

Five Little Ducks

Quack,

quack,

quack,

here we go—

Five little ducks in a long, long row.

· Turtle ·

There was a little turtle.
He lived in a box.

He swam in a puddle.
He climbed on the rocks.

He snapped at a mosquito.
He snapped at a flea.

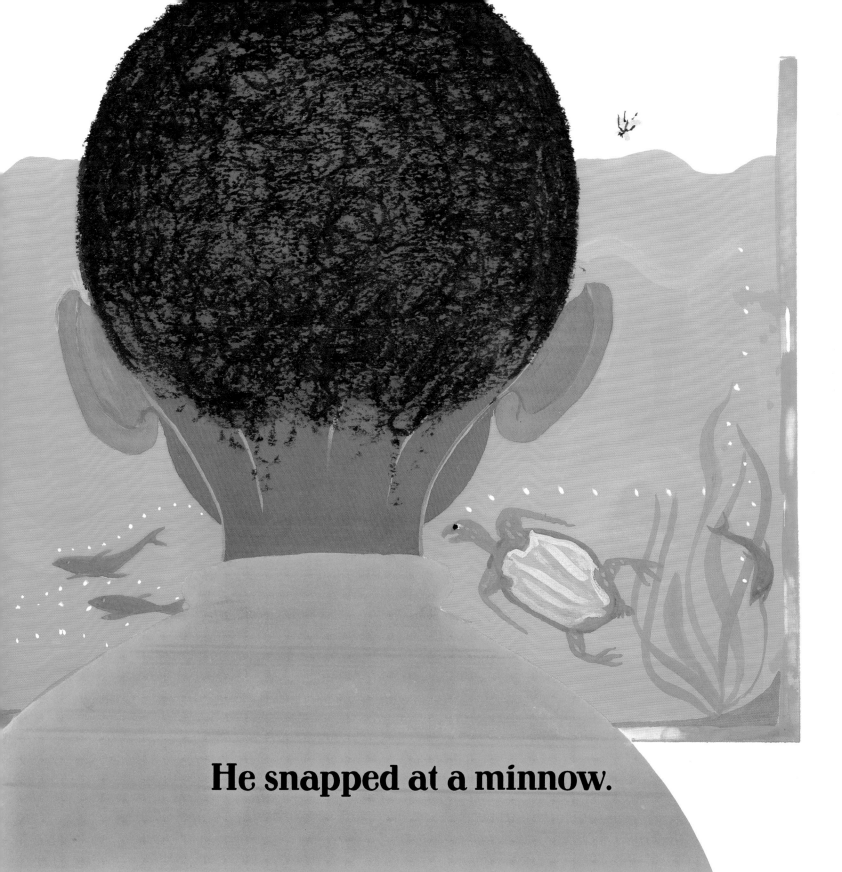

He snapped at a minnow.

And he snapped at me.

He caught the mosquito.
He caught the flea.

He caught the minnow....

But he didn't catch me!